P9-DEB-813

ONCE UPON A FAIRY TALE

The Snoring Princess

STORY BY
Anna Staniszewski

ART BY
Macky Pamintuan

BRANCHES

SCHOLASTIC INC.

ONCE UPON A FAIRY TALE

Help Kara and Zed fix all the fairy tales!

TABLE OF CONTENTS

For Lia — AS
For Ali, my brave princess — MP

If you purchased this book without a cover, you should be aware that this book is stolen property. It was reported as "unsold and destroyed" to the publisher, and neither the author nor the publisher has received any payment for this "stripped book."

Text copyright © 2020 by Anna Staniszewski
Illustrations © 2020 by Scholastic Inc.

Cover photos © Shutterstock: font (Idea Trader), stiches (KariDesign), texture (1028.art), (ailin1), (Hitdelight), (Tokarchuk Andrii), (vi mart).

All rights reserved. Published by Scholastic Inc., *Publishers since 1920*. SCHOLASTIC, BRANCHES, and associated logos are trademarks and/or registered trademarks of Scholastic Inc.

The publisher does not have any control over and does not assume any responsibility for author or third-party websites or their content.

No part of this publication may be reproduced, stored in a retrieval system, or transmitted in any form or by any means, electronic, mechanical, photocopying, recording, or otherwise, without written permission of the publisher. For information regarding permission, write to Scholastic Inc., Attention: Permissions Department, 557 Broadway, New York, NY 10012.

This book is a work of fiction. Names, characters, places, and incidents are either the product of the author's imagination or are used fictitiously, and any resemblance to actual persons, living or dead, business establishments, events, or locales is entirely coincidental.

Library of Congress Cataloging-in-Publication Data

Names: Staniszewski, Anna, author. | Pamintuan, Macky, illustrator.
Title: The snoring princess / by Anna Staniszewski ; illustrated by Macky Pamintuan.
Description: First edition. | New York : Branches/Scholastic Inc., 2020. | Series: Once upon a fairy tale; 4 | Audience: Ages 6–8. | Audience: Grades 2–3. | Summary: Princess Rosa's palace has been under a sleeping spell for one hundred years, and the spell will end at sunset; but Princess Rosa sleepwalks and when Kara and Zed enter the palace they find that she is missing—and the two fairies, Miranda and her son Leon, that have been caring for the sleepers do not seem particularly anxious to find her before the spell resets for another hundred years.
Identifiers: LCCN 2019034554 (print) | LCCN 2019034555 (ebook) | ISBN 9781338349818 (paperback) | ISBN 9781338349825 (hardcover) | ISBN 9781338349832 (ebk)
Subjects: LCSH: Sleeping Beauty (Tale)—Adaptations. | Princesses—Juvenile fiction. | Missing persons—Juvenile fiction. | Fairies—Juvenile fiction. | Magic—Juvenile fiction. | Fantasy. | CYAC: Characters in literature—Fiction. | Princesses—Fiction. | Missing persons—Fiction. | Fairies—Fiction. | Magic—Fiction. | LCGFT: Fantasy fiction.
Classification: LCC PZ7.S78685 Sn 2020 (print) | DDC 813.6 [Fic]—dc23
LC record available at https://lccn.loc.gov/2019034554

10 9 8 7 6 5 4 3 2 1   20 21 22 23 24

Printed in China   62
First edition, August 2020
Illustrated by Macky Pamintuan
Book design by Sarah Dvojack

The Missing Bag

It was almost spring. Kara was hard at work at her parents' shoe shop. She was swapping boots for sandals in a display case—and dreaming of adventure—when the bell on the front door jingled. Kara peered over a shelf. Her best friend, Zed, stepped into the shop with a small pig on a leash.

"Did you get *another* new pet?" Kara asked with a laugh. Zed was always taking in stray animals.

"No. This is Daisy. A witch let me borrow her," Zed said. "Daisy has the best nose in the Enchanted Kingdom. She's going to find my royal messenger bag."

Kara gasped. "Your bag is missing?" she asked. Zed's magic bag was how he delivered letters to kings and princesses throughout the land.

Zed scratched his head, looking worried. "Yes. Or, well, I can't remember where I left it," he said. "If I don't find it soon, I could lose my job!"

"I'll help you look," Kara said. She went over to her parents, who were busy dusting shelves. "Mom, Dad, is it okay if I go with Zed to find his bag?"

"Of course," her mother said.

"It sounds like Zed needs your help more than we do," her father added.

Kara loaded up her own bag with supplies. Then she, Zed, and Daisy hurried out of the shop.

"All right, Daisy," Zed said. "Use your amazing nose to find my messenger bag!"

Daisy sniffed the ground and tugged on her leash. Kara and Zed followed her through the village market. She stopped at a food stall where a goblin was selling cakes.

"I think she brought us here because she's hungry," Kara said with a sigh.

4

"No, I came here yesterday!" Zed said, grinning. "Daisy, if you find my bag, I'll give you one of Gram's cheesecakes!"

Daisy snorted and went back to sniffing the ground.

At that moment, Kara spotted a green tower deep in the forest, among the trees. She stepped away from the market to get a better look. She realized the tower wasn't *really* green. It was covered in thick vines.

"Zed!" Kara cried, waving him over. "I think that's Princess Rosa's palace!" She recognized it from a book she'd read about the Enchanted Kingdom's royal families. "Let's go take a look!"

She grabbed Zed's arm and started pulling him and Daisy into the forest.

"Who's Princess Rosa?" Zed asked as they walked.

"She's the princess who was cursed by an evil fairy when she pricked her finger on a sewing needle," Kara explained. "The curse made her fall into a deep sleep for one hundred years. A good fairy tried to help, but she couldn't break the curse. So she cast a sleeping spell on the *whole* palace instead. That way Princess Rosa would still have everyone with her when she woke up."

They came to a road covered in vines—just like the tower. As they followed it, the vines grew thicker and thicker.

"When is everyone supposed to wake up? Has it been one hundred years yet?" Zed asked.

Before Kara could answer, they heard someone shouting: "You're supposed to help me!" It was coming from the palace!

"It sounds like *someone* is awake," Zed pointed out.

Kara smiled. "And it sounds like they might need our help!"

2 In the Tower

Kara and Zed fought through vines on their way to the palace. Finally they came to the front door. It was wide open. Two guards were sleeping on cots nearby.

Daisy tugged on her leash, trying to go back the way they had come.

"I think Daisy's right," Zed said. "We should keep looking for my messenger bag."

"We will," Kara promised. "But first let's make sure everyone here is all right."

Zed looked nervous, but he nodded.

They tiptoed inside. Everywhere they looked, people were snoring. The palace was still tidy, though. There was no dust or dirt in sight.

"I wish I lived here," Zed whispered as they went through a ballroom lined with beds. "Then I could sleep as much as I wanted."

"You'd also be over one hundred years old," Kara whispered back. She was surprised to see that some of the people sleeping in the ballroom had mustaches or cat whiskers drawn on their faces.

Someone has been having a little fun, Kara thought.

They both froze as a loud thud echoed above their heads.

"I think it came from inside the tower," Kara said. She waved for Zed and Daisy to follow her up the staircase. As they climbed, snores echoed from inside every room.

At the top of the tower, they found a bedroom that sparkled with gold and silver. Even the hair ribbons by the mirror gleamed.

"This must be Princess Rosa's room," Kara whispered.

But when they tiptoed over to the bed, they didn't find a sleeping princess. They found a boy. He was about their age with pointy ears and wings—and he was awake!

"Who are you?" Kara asked.

"*Shh!*" the boy said, sitting up. "You don't want Mother to find out you're here!"

"Who's your mother?" Zed asked.

"I'm Leon. My mother, Miranda, and I are the fairies who take care of the palace and everyone in it," Leon answered as he hopped out of bed.

Kara was surprised that Leon was nearly as tall as she was. "I thought all fairies were tiny," she said.

"Fairies can actually change shape and size," Leon said. "It's one of our magic powers." He looked Kara and Zed over curiously. "Who are *you*?"

"I'm Zed, a royal messenger," Zed answered. "This is my friend Kara and our pig, Daisy."

Daisy let out a loud snort.

"Why are you here?" Leon asked.

"We heard shouting from the road and thought someone might need our help," Kara explained.

"That was Mother yelling at me for drawing on people when I'm supposed to be helping her clean," Leon said.

"*You* did that?" Zed asked with a chuckle.

Leon shrugged. "It gets a little boring here sometimes."

"But, wait," Kara said, looking around the sparkling room. "Where's Princess Rosa? This is her bedroom. Shouldn't she be in her bed?"

"Oh, well, you see," Leon said slowly. "It's just that Princess Rosa . . . she . . . she's gone."

Another Hundred Years

"**P**rincess Rosa is *missing*?" Kara cried.

"She's not *missing*," Leon said. "She just . . . left the palace."

"When did you last see her?" Zed asked.

"Last night," Leon said. "But this morning, she wasn't in her bed. And her slippers and robe were gone, too."

"But why is the princess awake?" Kara asked. "Everyone else is still asleep." She could hear them snoring below like a whistling orchestra.

"I—I don't know, but the sleeping spell is supposed to end at sunset," Leon explained. His wings twitched, as if he were nervous. "If the princess isn't back in the palace by tonight, then the  spell will start all over again."

"Everyone will have to sleep for *another* one hundred years?" Zed asked.

"Oh no! We need to find her!" Kara said.

Just then, a voice called up the stairs: "Leon! Are you up there?" It was the same one that Kara and Zed had heard yelling from outside.

A moment later, a woman appeared in the doorway. She had large wings and long, silver hair. This had to be Leon's mother, Miranda.

Miranda's eyes widened when she saw Kara and Zed. "What are these humans doing here?" she asked Leon.

"They heard you shouting and came to make sure everything was all right," Leon explained. Then he added, more slowly, "They were asking about the princess."

"We're ready to help!" Kara jumped in.

"We are?" Zed asked.

"Yes!" Kara cried. She was always up for an adventure. "We'll find Princess Rosa and bring her back to the palace before sunset!"

Find the Princess

"**K**ara," Zed said. "If we go look for Princess Rosa, we won't have time to find my messenger bag."

"Maybe Daisy can help us find both," Kara said. "Her nose is magical, right?"

Zed's face lit up. "That's true!" he said. He turned to Miranda and Leon. "We *will* help you find the princess!"

"Thank you," Miranda replied. "But Leon and I can manage on our own."

"Zed and I really *can* help," Kara said. "We solve mysteries all the time!"

"Don't bother trying to talk her out of it," Zed told Miranda. "Kara loves adventures."

"Maybe we *should* let them help, Mother," Leon added. "The princess has been gone a long time. She's never—"

"Very well," Miranda cut in. "You three go search for Princess Rosa. I will stay here in case she comes back."

"You want m-m-me to go with them?" Leon asked, sounding surprised.

"Yes," Miranda said. "Let's go pack for your adventure."

As the fairies left the room, Miranda whispered in Leon's ear. His wings drooped. *Is Miranda scolding him again?* Kara wondered.

When they were gone, Kara looked around the room for clues about where the princess might have gone. But other than a few books she'd love to read, Kara found nothing.

A few minutes later, Leon and Miranda came back. The group headed down the tower steps, past the snoring residents of the palace.

"Daisy, forget about my messenger bag for now. Find Princess Rosa first!" Zed said.

Daisy sniffed the floor. Then she pulled them out through the front door of the palace.

"Good luck," Miranda called as she closed the front door behind them. Kara heard it lock with a sharp *click*.

The pig kept pulling her leash until she brought Kara, Zed, and Leon to a fountain in the palace courtyard. She stood near the bubbling water, tugging and squealing.

"Daisy can smell that Princess Rosa came this way," Zed explained. He started to climb into the shallow water.

"Wait, can't we go *around* the fountain?" Kara asked.

Zed shook his head. "If Daisy wants us to go this way, then we need to go this way."

Kara groaned. "Fine. We'll follow Daisy's nose. But your pig better be right!"

Kara and Zed sloshed through the fountain as Leon fluttered over it on his small wings. Then they headed toward the road, leaving three sets of wet footprints behind.

"You'll see," Zed said cheerfully. "Daisy will bring us right to the princess!"

A Pet Butterfly?

Daisy did *not* bring them right to Princess Rosa. After they left the palace grounds, she led them to a farmer's field, where she nibbled on some corn.

"I think she's following her stomach instead of her nose again," Kara said.

"Remember," Zed told Daisy, "there's some cheesecake waiting for you at home."

That got Daisy's attention. She led the group back into the forest. As they searched for any sign of the princess, the early-afternoon sun grew brighter. Kara took a sun hat out of her bag and put it on.

A minute later, Leon raised his hands and wiggled his fingers. Sparks of magic danced between his fingertips. Then a small sun hat appeared in Leon's hands!

Kara and Zed both gasped.

"With Daisy's nose and your magic, it'll be easy to find the princess!" Zed told Leon.

Leon's wings drooped again. "My magic is only strong enough to do small things like make hats," he said. "It's not like Mother's. She can do anything." When he put the hat on his head, it was crooked and lumpy. "After the sleeping spell ends, I won't have to help at the palace anymore. Then I want to work as a royal messenger like you, Zed. You don't need any magic for that."

Zed's face lit up. "That's true!" Then his smile faded. "You just have to make sure *not* to lose your messenger bag . . ."

"Don't worry," Kara told her friend. "We'll find it."

Something small fluttered over and landed on Leon's shoulder. Its wings sparkled in the sun. Leon seemed to listen to it for a moment, frowning. Then it flew away again.

"What was that?" Kara asked.

"Oh, it was . . ." Leon said, "my pet butterfly."

"You have a pet butterfly? That's so cool!" Zed cried. "How do *I* get one of those?"

"Sorry," Leon said. "Only, uh, fairies have them."

"Oh," Zed said with a sigh. "How long have you had your pet butterfly?"

Before Leon could answer, Daisy broke in with an excited squeal. She dragged Zed over to a tree.

"What do you have there, Daisy?" Zed asked. He picked up a piece of gold fabric.

Kara hurried over. "That's a hair ribbon," she said. "Princess Rosa has others just like it in her bedroom. Right, Leon?"

Leon was quiet for a moment. "I th-think so," he said finally.

"See? We *are* going the right way!" Zed said.

Kara shook her head in wonder. *Maybe Daisy's nose really is magical!* she thought.

6
Achoo!

Kara, Zed, and Leon followed Daisy through the forest as she sniffed for more clues about where Princess Rosa had gone. Soon they were trudging through deep mud. Finally Daisy led them to the edge of a pond.

"She's not going to make us swim, is she?" Kara asked.

Three large frogs popped their heads out of the mud.

"Keep it down!" one of the frogs croaked. "It's not spring yet!"

"Sorry," Zed called back.

"Why do people keep waking us up?" another frog squawked.

"*People?* Wait! Did you see a princess come by here?" Kara asked the frogs.

"No, but this morning, we heard someone sawing trees right above our heads," the first one grumbled. "So rude!"

"Sawing trees?" Zed repeated.

Kara looked around. "I don't see any newly cut trees," she said.

The frogs didn't answer. They had already settled back in the mud, asleep.

"We must have made a wrong turn," Leon said. "Let's turn around."

But Kara wasn't going to give up so easily. "Let's take a break and have lunch," she said. "Then we'll follow this path a little farther."

They sat on a large rock and unpacked the food they had brought. Daisy dove right in.

"No, Daisy!" Zed cried, shooing her away. "Save some food for the rest of us."

Just then, Leon's pet butterfly fluttered over again. Leon seemed to listen to it before it flew away.

"Can your butterfly talk?" Zed asked.

But Leon didn't answer. Instead he got up and went over to a nearby bush. "Maybe we should pick some of these berries for Daisy," Leon said.

"Good idea," Kara said.

They gathered handfuls of berries, and Daisy gobbled them up.

Zed had a few, too. "Delicious!" he exclaimed.

When everyone's bellies were full, they set off again, with Daisy in the lead. They'd gone only a little ways when—**ACHOO!** Daisy let out a loud sneeze. And another. And another.

Kara and Zed looked at each other. "Uh-oh," they said.

7

Footprints

As the group continued through the woods, Daisy kept sneezing.

"Is she getting sick?" Zed asked, wiping the pig's nose.

"It started after she ate those berries." Kara's eyes widened. "*They* must be what's making her sneeze!"

Soon the group came to a fork in the road. They had to choose one of two paths, but Daisy was sneezing worse than ever.

"Which way should we go?" Kara asked her friends.

"That way," Leon said, pointing to the left. "It has been traveled a lot more. See how the dirt is packed down?"

"Yes, but Daisy thinks we should go the other way," Zed said. The pig was pulling toward the path on the right.

"Her nose is stuffy," Leon pointed out. "She might be confused."

Kara looked back and forth between the two paths. It was already afternoon. Time was running out to find Rosa before the spell started over. They had to make a decision.

Suddenly, Kara spotted something in the dirt on the right-hand path. Footprints—and they looked fresh!

She kneeled down to get a closer look. The toes of the footprints were rounded, and the edges looked fuzzy. "These prints were made by someone wearing slippers," Kara said. "It has to be Princess Rosa!"

"How can you tell what kind of shoes they came from?" Leon asked.

"Kara's parents own a shoe shop," Zed explained. "She knows shoes better than anyone."

"Oh," Leon said, sounding disappointed.

"Aren't you glad we found another clue?" Zed asked.

"Of c-course I am!" Leon said, his cheeks turning pink.

Kara pointed to the path on the right. "Princess Rosa went *this* way," she said. "Let's go!"

The Cliff

Kara had been sure the path would bring them to Princess Rosa. But a few minutes later, it ended at the bottom of a rocky cliff.

"There's no way Princess Rosa climbed *this* in her slippers," Leon said. "We should turn back and take the other path."

Kara sighed. "I was so sure those footprints were Princess Rosa's," she said.

Just then, a loud sound echoed above their heads. It sounded like a saw.

REEERAAAW!

"That's strange. Someone must be cutting down trees on top of this cliff," Zed said.

"Wait," Kara said. "Remember what the frogs told us? They were woken up by the sound of someone sawing trees."

"Maybe we're following a lumberjack instead of a princess," Zed joked.

"Let's turn back," Leon urged again. "We're running out of time."

But Kara shook her head. Something didn't add up. "No, we need to climb up and see where that sound is coming from," she said.

"Climb up *there*?" Zed cried. He looked a little sick at the thought.

"You can stay down here," Kara told him. "Someone should be with Daisy anyway." She turned to Leon. "And you can fly up with me."

Leon's eyes widened. "But—"

"Come on, let's go!" Kara said. She went over to the cliff and began to climb. And climb. And climb.

The Snoring Princess

The sawing sound grew louder as Kara neared the top of the cliff. **REEERAAAW!** Below her, Leon struggled to keep up on his small wings.

Finally Kara reached the top of the cliff. She flopped down on the grass to catch her breath. A moment later, Leon flew up and landed heavily next to her.

When Kara stood up, she spotted a clump of scraggly bushes. A young woman was curled up among them. Her clothes were covered in mud, and her slippers were nearly falling apart.

"Princess Rosa!" Kara cried. She hurried over to the princess with Leon following behind.

The sawing sound came again. **REEERAAAW!**

Kara gasped. The sound was coming from the princess's nose. No one was cutting down trees. Princess Rosa was *snoring*! She was sound asleep!

"Is she all right?" Leon asked.

"Yes, but she must have fallen asleep again," Kara said. "I'm surprised she can sleep through her snoring."

Suddenly, Princess Rosa sat up.

Kara jumped back. "Your Highness!" she said, dipping into a bow. "We're sorry to wake you!"

But the princess's eyes remained closed. She let out another giant snore. **REEERAAAW!**

Kara stared in disbelief. Princess Rosa was still sleeping!

The princess got to her feet and started stumbling around.

"Leon, she's sleepwalking!" Kara said. "Help me get her back down the cliff safely!"

But Leon didn't move. "M-my wings aren't strong enough to carry her," he said.

"Then climb down with me instead of flying," Kara said. "Please, I need your help!"

"I-I can't . . ." Leon stammered. For some reason, he sounded miserable.

Kara turned back to the princess and gasped. Princess Rosa was at the edge of the cliff!

"Princess Rosa, no!" Kara cried. "You'll fall!"

10

Shortcut

Kara watched, amazed, as the princess easily climbed down the cliff—as if she'd done it before. She kept snoring the whole way. **REEERAAAW!**

After a minute, Kara followed her. Leon fluttered behind them like a giant butterfly.

When Kara was on solid ground again, she found Princess Rosa snoring in a pile of leaves. **REEERAAAW!**

Zed stood nearby grinning. "And I thought my gram's snores were loud!" he said. "How did Princess Rosa get *here*?"

"She must have sleepwalked right out of her bedroom, all the way to the top of that cliff," Kara said. She glanced at the sun. It was getting lower in the sky. "We need to get her back to the palace right away!"

Kara and Leon gently pulled Princess Rosa to her feet. But leading her was slow work. The princess would walk a few steps and then flop on the ground. Even with Zed and Daisy's help, it was still taking too long.

Finally they made it back to the fork in the road.

As the princess flopped on the ground yet again, Leon's pet butterfly fluttered over. Kara could hear its tiny voice whispering in Leon's ear, but she  couldn't make out what it was saying. Then it flew away.

There is something strange about that butterfly, Kara thought. She turned to Leon and asked, "What did your butterfly just tell you?"

"Oh, it reminded me about . . . a shortcut to the palace," Leon said.

"A shortcut?" Zed asked, his face brightening. "We could use one of those right now!"

"There's a secret trail that way," Leon said, pointing through some thick trees.

"That doesn't seem like the right direction . . ." Kara said. Leon had acted so strangely up on the cliff. She wasn't sure if she should trust him or not. "I'll check my map."

Leon shook his head. "We don't have time for that. We need to get back to the palace."

"He's right," Zed said. "We can't let the princess sleep for another hundred years!"

Kara sighed. "All right. Let's try taking the shortcut. But we have to hurry!"

Up the River

The journey through the forest was still slow with Leon's shortcut. The princess kept trying to wander away, and her snores were so loud, Kara's ears were ringing. **REEERAAAW!** At least Daisy had stopped sneezing.

Finally Kara noticed the trees thinning up ahead. *Maybe we're coming to the road that leads to the palace*, she thought.

When they got closer, Kara realized there wasn't a road. It was a river!

"How are we supposed to get across?" Zed asked, staring at the rushing water.

Kara turned to Leon. "I thought you said this was a shortcut," she said.

"It is," he insisted. "I'll just make a boat with my magic. The river will bring us right to the palace."

"I don't remember there being a river near the palace," Kara said. She grabbed Princess Rosa's arm to keep her from wandering off again.

"It—it's behind the palace," Leon said. "That's why you didn't see it earlier."

"But how will you make a boat? I thought you said your magic was barely strong enough to make a hat," Kara pressed. *Something strange is definitely going on here*, she thought.

"Kara," Zed cut in.
"Leon is just trying to
help. And look! You can
see the palace right over
there." He pointed to a
vine-covered tower peeking

out from the trees, farther down the river.

"All right," Kara agreed. Still, she kept a close eye on Leon as he began to work his magic.

Leon held his hands over the water and wiggled his fingers again. Sparks began to fly from his fingertips.

Slowly, the bottom of a boat appeared. Then the sides. Then the oars. Then the anchor.

Finally the magic sparks faded. "The boat is ready," Leon said.

Kara let go of Princess Rosa's arm and went over to take a look. The boat was lopsided as it sat in the water. "Those oars are awfully small," she pointed out.

Just then there was a loud *splash!*

"Kara, behind you!" Zed cried.

Kara spun around. Princess Rosa was no longer by her side. She had fallen into the river!

12
Wrong Way!

Kara stared down the river in shock. Princess Rosa was floating away!

"We need to go after her!" Zed cried.

Kara leaped into the boat. Leon, Zed, and Daisy jumped in after her.

The boat swayed and creaked, but it stayed afloat. Leon pulled up the anchor as Kara and Zed grabbed the oars. Ahead of them, Princess Rosa floated along on her back with the current. She was still snoring. **REEERAAAW!**

"Wow, the princess can really sleep through *anything*," Zed said.

They barely needed the tiny oars. The current was strong, and it helped bring them to Princess Rosa. Kara and Zed kept the boat steady as Leon fished her out of the water.

When the princess was on board, Kara breathed a sigh of relief. Princess Rosa was safe, and the palace was so close they could see it. They were going to make it back before sunset. The sleeping spell would be broken at last!

But when Kara glanced at Leon, she noticed a grim look on his face.

"What's the matter?" Kara asked, but Leon only shook his head.

"Wait," Zed said suddenly. "The palace is getting smaller. The current is bringing us the wrong way!"

"We need to paddle against it!" Kara cried.

They rowed as hard as they could, but it only turned the boat around. Now they were heading farther from the palace *and* facing the wrong way. Exhausted, Kara and Zed put down their oars.

"We'll have to jump out and swim to shore," Zed said. "Pigs are great swimmers. Maybe Daisy can pull the princess along?"

Kara shook her head. "No, we're all staying in this boat. We can't risk losing track of the princess again. Plus, the current is too strong for us to swim."

"Then what do we do?" Zed asked.

"I don't know," she admitted. "But we have to think of something. We're running out of time!"

Just then, Leon's pet butterfly landed on his shoulder.

Kara was able to catch a few whispered words: ". . . the palace . . . sunset . . . boat . . . "

Wait, I know that voice! Kara thought.

13
The Whole Truth

The butterfly started to fly away, but Kara caught it in her hand.

"No, don't!" Leon cried.

Kara opened her fingers to peek at the creature. It was small and had wings like a butterfly, but its face . . .

"It's Miranda!" Kara said with a gasp.

"Release me!" Miranda shouted in a tiny voice.

Then she shot red sparks at Kara's fingers.

"Ouch!" Kara cried, letting her go.

Miranda fluttered away from the boat and disappeared into the forest.

Zed's mouth was open in surprise. "Wait," he said to Leon. "So you *don't* have a pet butterfly?"

Leon hid his face in his hands. "No," he said through his fingers.

"Tell us what's really going on, Leon," Kara ordered as the palace got farther away. "And hurry!"

Leon took a deep breath. "Princess Rosa has been sleepwalking in and out of the palace for years," he began. "We leave the door unlocked for her, and she always comes back safely after a little while. But this morning, it had been hours and Princess Rosa still wasn't back. I was getting worried."

"Then Zed and I showed up," Kara said.

Leon nodded. "I wanted to tell you both the truth," he said. "But Mother made me promise to always keep Princess Rosa's sleepwalking a secret. She doesn't want people to think we're bad at our jobs."

"That's why Miranda didn't want our help finding the princess," Zed said.

But Miranda did *agree to let us help*, Kara thought. *It doesn't make sense. Unless . . .*

"Miranda made you tag along to *stop us* from finding the princess, didn't she?" Kara asked Leon. That explained why he kept suggesting they should turn back.

"Yes," Leon admitted. "Mother used her magic to make herself look like a butterfly so she could follow us. She told me those berries would make Daisy sneeze. And it was her idea to bring you to the river and pretend it was a shortcut."

"But why would Miranda do all of this?" Zed asked. "If we don't get Princess Rosa back to the palace, the sleeping spell will go on for another one hundred years!"

Kara thought back to what Leon had said about leaving the door unlocked for the princess. But then she remembered the *click!* of Miranda locking the palace door behind them.

The pieces of the puzzle slid into place. "Because," Kara said, "Miranda loves her job so much that she doesn't want the spell to end!"

14
Going Upstream

"**I**s that true?" Zed asked Leon, his eyes wide. "Does Miranda *want* the sleeping spell to start over?"

Leon nodded. "Yes. My great-grandmother was the good fairy who cast the sleeping spell on the palace in the first place. Mother grew up there, and she took over the job when she was old enough," he explained. "She's worked hard to keep everyone in the palace safe. If the spell ends, we'll have to leave."

Kara looked at Zed. She could tell that he felt bad for Miranda like she did.

"I love the palace, too," Leon added. "But my mother can't imagine living anywhere else."

"That must be hard, but we cannot trap everyone in a deep sleep for another one hundred years," Kara said.

"If we did, then you'd never become a royal messenger," Zed told Leon.

"I know," Leon said, his wings drooping lower than ever. "But Mother's plan worked. We'll never get back to the palace before the sun sets now."

Kara could see only the very top of the palace above the trees as their boat continued to rush down the river. "Were you telling the truth when you said the river runs behind the palace?" she asked.

"Yes," Leon said, "but it doesn't matter. The current is taking us the wrong way!"

"With some help from your magic, we might be able to row against it," Kara said.

"You've seen my magic," Leon said. "It's not strong enough."

"Please, Leon," Kara said. "We can't do this without you."

Leon took a shaky breath. Then he raised his hands. As he wiggled his fingers, sparks appeared in the air.

Kara felt the boat slow down. But the current was still bringing them the wrong way.

"I can't do it," Leon said, shaking his head.

"Keep trying," Kara urged.

Zed picked up his oar again. "We'll help!"

Leon nodded and closed his eyes. The sparks between his fingers grew brighter. The boat slowed down and started moving backward, against the current.

"Paddle!" Kara called to Zed.

The current was strong, but with Leon's magical push, they fought through it. Soon the boat was moving toward the palace.

But it wasn't enough. They were still going too slowly.

"The sun is setting," Zed cried. "We'll never make it!"

"We can't give up," Kara said. She tried to think. If only Daisy could paddle, too.

Wait.

Kara sucked in an excited breath. "Zed," she said. "Is Daisy *really* a good swimmer?"

"All pigs are excellent swimmers," he said. "Why?"

Kara smiled. "Because I have an idea."

The Right Thing

Kara quickly explained her plan to Zed and Leon. Then she tied Daisy's leash to the front of the boat.

"Daisy, find Princess Rosa's palace!" Zed told her.

Daisy jumped into the river. She started swimming, pulling the boat behind her. Kara and Zed grabbed their oars again while Leon wiggled his fingers to call his magic.

With everyone working together, the boat easily turned and moved against the current. Soon, they reached the riverbank behind the palace.

Zed helped Daisy out of the water. She looked wet and happy. Meanwhile, Kara and Leon led Princess Rosa from the boat.

The group rushed up the path and around to the front of the palace, where Leon unlocked the door. They all hurried inside and led Princess Rosa to her bedroom in the top of the tower.

Outside, the last rays of sunlight were fading away.

"We made it!" Kara cried.

As they put Princess Rosa back in bed, Miranda appeared in the doorway. "How did you get here?" the fairy cried. She turned to Leon. "You were supposed to keep them from bringing the princess back!"

"I had to help Kara and Zed break the spell, Mother," he said. "It was the right thing to do."

"Is it *right* that we're going to lose our home and our jobs?" Miranda demanded. There were tears in her eyes.

Suddenly, a sleepy voice came from behind them: "What is all this yelling?"

Everyone spun around to find Princess Rosa sitting up in bed. Her eyes were wide open.

The sleeping spell was over.

"Princess Rosa, you're awake!" Miranda cried, sinking into a low bow.

"Who are you?" the princess asked. "What happened? And why am I all muddy?"

Rise and Shine

Kara and Zed told Princess Rosa about the curse that had been put on her and about the spell on the palace. They also told her about her sleepwalking through the muddy forest and Miranda's sneaky plan.

"I'm sorry, Your Highness," Miranda said, bursting into tears. "I just didn't want to ever leave the palace—or you!"

The sound of dozens of groggy voices began drifting up from downstairs.

"What happened?"

"I'm starving!"

"I really need to use the bathroom!"

Princess Rosa got out of bed. "This palace is full of people who need looking after," she said. "Miranda, your family has cared for us all these long, sleepy years. Will you and your son stay on as the official palace housekeepers?"

"Of course, Your Highness!" Miranda cried. "We would be honored."

But Leon didn't look happy at the idea. "Mother," he said. "I don't want to work at the palace anymore. I want to see the world and be a royal messenger like Zed."

"What?" Miranda asked. "Why didn't you tell me this before?"

"I didn't think you'd listen. You were so focused on us staying at the palace," Leon said.

"I wanted you to be as happy in the palace as I was. Of course I won't force you to stay here!" Miranda said. She gave her son a warm hug. "You'll make a wonderful royal messenger."

Leon's eyes widened in surprise. "Really? Thank you!" he said. "And I can still help out from time to time."

Miranda nodded. "Thank you, Leon. Now, if you'll all excuse me, I have a job to do!" She hurried out of the room, her wings fluttering with excitement.

"Wait, I'll give you a hand!" Leon called after her. He gave Kara and Zed a grin of thanks and then flew off.

Princess Rosa let out a loud yawn. "I'm so tired," she said. "I feel as though I've been walking for ages!" She crawled back into bed and pulled up the covers. In a minute, she was asleep again—but this time, just for a while.

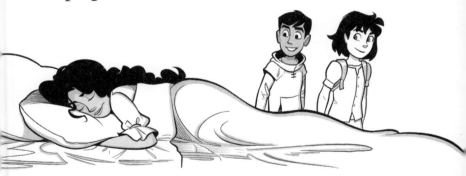

Kara and Zed tiptoed down the tower steps, with Daisy trailing after them.

Downstairs, the palace was bustling with life again. People were stretching, drinking coffee, and talking about the dreams they'd had over the past one hundred years.

Miranda and Leon seemed right at home as they fluttered around, preparing a breakfast feast for everyone.

Kara and Zed looked at each other and smiled. It was time for them to go home.

As they left the palace, Kara took a lantern out of her bag. Then she and Zed headed back along the road with Daisy happily sniffing the ground again.

When they finally came to Zed's cottage, the sweet smell of Gram's cheesecake wafted through the window.

Daisy let out a sudden snort and pulled Zed over to the front gate. Zed's messenger bag was hanging on a nail.

"Oh!" Zed said. "I forgot I left it out here yesterday."

Kara laughed. "It's a good thing you had Daisy to help you find it," she said.

"Well, my bag has been found," Zed said. "I guess our adventure is over!"

"At least for today," Kara said with a smile. "Now let's go have some dessert."

About the Creators

Anna Staniszewski is the author of over a dozen books for young readers, including *Secondhand Wishes* and *Dogosauraus Rex*. She lives outside of Boston with her family and teaches at Simmons University. She shares both Kara's love of reading and Zed's love of dessert.

Macky Pamintuan was born in the Philippines. He received his bachelor of fine arts in San Francisco, and he has illustrated numerous children's books. He has a smarty-pants young daughter who loves to read and go on imaginary adventures with her furry pal and trusty sidekick, Winter. He now lives in Mexico with his family.

Once Upon a Fairy Tale

The Snoring Princess

Questions and Activities

Leon tries to stop Kara and Zed from finding Princess Rosa. But Kara doesn't give up! Name two of the clues Kara and Zed find that lead them to the princess.

In chapter 6, how does Leon stop Daisy from using her magic nose to follow Princess Rosa's scent?

Why does Miranda want the sleeping spell to start over again? Why does Leon want it to end? Reread chapters 13 and 14 to find the answers.

Before Kara and Zed start looking for Princess Rosa, they are looking for Zed's missing messenger bag. Where is his bag found at the end of the story? And who finds it?

Imagine *you* have fairy magic. Can you change shape, like Miranda? Can you create things, like Leon? Draw a picture to show how you use your magic powers.

scholastic.com/branches